Dealing with Challenges

Anxiety

By Meg Gaertner

www.littlebluehousebooks.com

Copyright © 2022 by Little Blue House, Mendota Heights, MN 55120. All rights reserved. No part of this book may be reproduced or utilized in any form or by any means without written permission from the publisher.

Little Blue House is distributed by North Star Editions:
sales@northstareditions.com | 888-417-0195

Produced for Little Blue House by Red Line Editorial.

Photographs ©: Shutterstock Images, cover, 9, 11, 12, 17 (top), 17 (bottom), 19, 20, 23, 24 (top left), 24 (top right), 24 (bottom left), 24 (bottom right); iStockphoto, 4, 7, 15

Library of Congress Control Number: 2021916734

ISBN
978-1-64619-481-0 (hardcover)
978-1-64619-508-4 (paperback)
978-1-64619-560-2 (ebook pdf)
978-1-64619-535-0 (hosted ebook)

Printed in the United States of America
Mankato, MN
012022

About the Author

Meg Gaertner enjoys reading, writing, dancing, and being outside. She lives in Minnesota.

Table of Contents

Anxiety **5**

Feeling Better **13**

Too Much **21**

Glossary **24**

Index **24**

Anxiety

A girl has a hard test tomorrow.

She worries about doing well.

A boy goes to a new school.

He worries about making friends.

Anxiety is a feeling of fear
or worry.

Everyone worries sometimes.

The feeling often goes away
over time.

You might feel anxiety in your body.
Your heart might beat quickly.
Your head might hurt.

Feeling Better

If you feel anxiety, find a quiet place.

Slow down and breathe deeply.

This will help your thoughts slow

down, too.

Walk outside in the fresh air.

Nature can be peaceful.

Notice what you can see and hear.

Notice what you can touch and smell.

Take care of your body.

Eat fruits and vegetables.

Get good sleep, and

exercise often.

fruits and vegetables

sleep

Know that you are not alone.

Share your feelings with

your family.

Or talk to your teacher at school.

Too Much

Sometimes anxiety becomes too much.

People can't stop thinking or worrying.

They have trouble sleeping or doing everyday work.

People can still get help.

They can talk to a therapist.

This person can teach ways of

handling anxiety.

Glossary

fruits and vegetables

sleep

nature

therapist

Index

B
breathing, 13

N
nature, 14

S
sleep, 16, 21

T
therapist, 22